# INTRODUCTION

To the readers of this book:

There are many questions that you will be asked as you travel through this earth,
but none is as important as this one
'Who am I?"
Start asking it now and write down your answers. There is room in this book for your answers
and pictures. Years from now you will be interested to see what you have written.
We hope that you enjoy answering the questions and that you will add some of your own. If you
would like to send one of your pictures for use in a future edition of this book, please wrap it
carefully so it won't get bent of damaged in the mail. Send it to:
Shirley Ann Burbank/Who am I?

P.O. Box 2466
Ellicott City, M D 21041

On the back of your picture please put this information:

Your name
Your address & phone number

# Instructions for teachers who use this book:

You can use this poem with even very young children by reading it to them and letting them draw their own pictures on the blank page. That is why the book opens flat.

Parents are teachers and the pictures drawn by 3 & 4 year olds will be fun to have later. There are pages in the back for one student to keep a record of his growth as the years go by. If the student can't write, the parent/teacher can write his answers for him until he can do it for himself.

This book can also be used in a classroom if each student has their own copy in which to record their pictures and answers to
Who am I?

The pictures in this first edition were collected by the author over about 20 years and were drawn by people of many ages from a four year old nephew to a lady in a retirement home.

Who am I?
How do I know who I am?
Can I tell by how I look?

There are enough shapes and colors of eyes, noses and mouths
To fill a book.

Hair can be many colors and fixed in many ways.

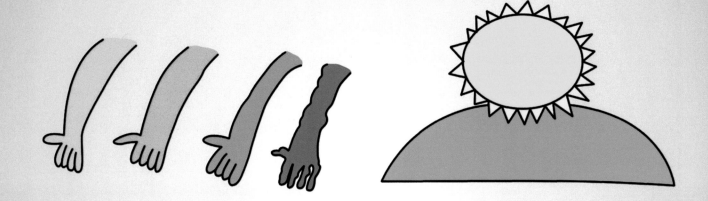

Skin can be light, dark, freckled, smooth or wrinkled.
It changes through the days.

I can be short, tall, wide, thin, strong or weak.

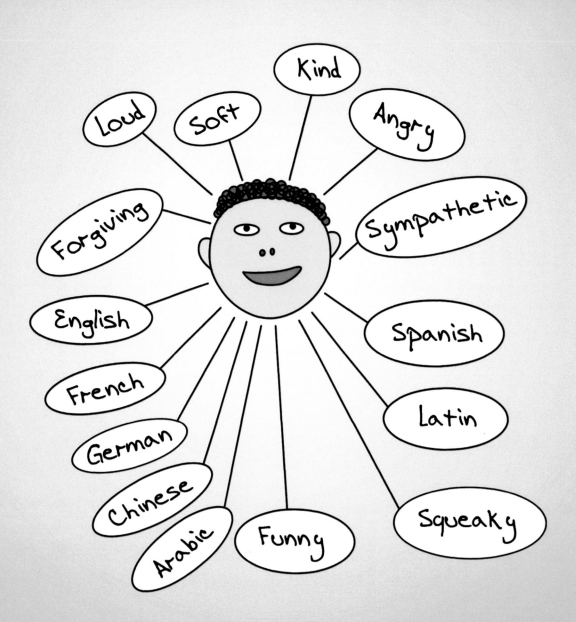

There are many voices with which I speak.

There are many ways that I can dress,
And I can choose which I like best.

My skin, my nose, my ears and eyes,
My mouth, my hair, my shape and size,
These are the things that others see.
But that's not necessarily me.

Within my heart and brain I know
There lives a me who wants to grow,

To learn about the world outside
And take from home and school a guide

For how to live a life of worth
Sharing with others on this earth.

I can choose from many a way
Just how to think and act each day.

Who I am is how I'll be.

You are you and I am me learning to live in harmony.

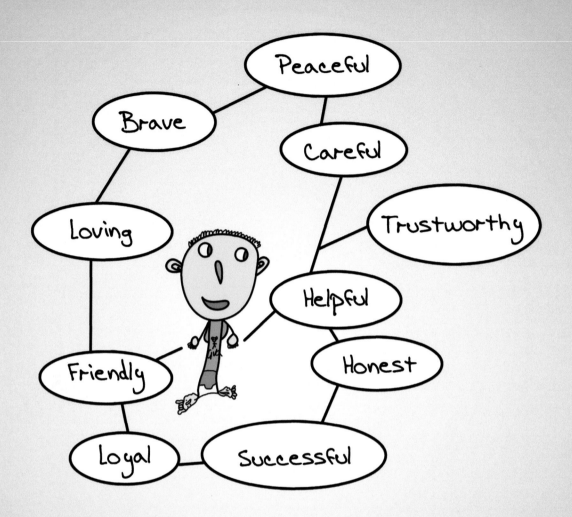

So ...
WHO AM I ?

Whatever I decide you'll see.
I can choose to be what I want to be!

Date_____          Who am I?

This is me.

My Name_____

My address_____

My phone number_____

Color of my hair_____ Color of my eyes_____

My height_____          My weight_____

Color of my skin_____

Voice with which I speak_____

My favorite clothes_____

Things I choose to be_____

Date_____          Who am I?

This is me.

My Name_____

My address_____

My phone number_____

Color of my hair_____ Color of my eyes_____

My height_____          My weight_____

Color of my skin_____

Voice with which I speak_____

My favorite clothes_____

Things I choose to be_____

Date_____          **Who am I?**

                             **This is me.**

My Name_____

My address_____

My phone number_____

Color of my hair_____ Color of my eyes_____

My height_____          My weight_____

Color of my skin_____

Voice with which I speak_____

My favorite clothes_____

Things I choose to be_____

Edwards Brothers,Inc!
Thorofare, NJ 08086
19 May, 2010
BA2010139